Gilroy Unified School District

ISBN: 9781424260560
Meet Vidia

Author: Sisler, Celeste
Copyright Year: 2015

WELCOME TO
PASSPORT TO READING
A beginning reader's ticket to a brand-new world!

Every book in this program is designed to build read-along and read-alone skills, level by level, through engaging and enriching stories. As the reader turns each page, he or she will become more confident with new vocabulary, sight words, and comprehension.

These PASSPORT TO READING levels will help you choose the perfect book for every reader.

READING TOGETHER
Read short words in simple sentence structures together to begin a reader's journey.

READING OUT LOUD
Encourage developing readers to sound out words in more complex stories with simple vocabulary.

READING INDEPENDENTLY
Newly independent readers gain confidence reading more complex sentences with higher word counts.

READY TO READ MORE
Readers prepare for chapter books with fewer illustrations and longer paragraphs.

This book features sight words from the educator-supported Dolch Sight Words List. This encourages the reader to recognize commonly used vocabulary words, increasing reading speed and fluency.

For more information, please visit passporttoreadingbooks.com.

Enjoy the journey!

Little, Brown and Company

Hachette Book Group
237 Park Avenue, New York, NY 10017
Visit our website at lb-kids.com

Little, Brown and Company is a division of Hachette Book Group, Inc. The Little, Brown name and logo are trademarks of Hachette Book Group, Inc.

The publisher is not responsible for websites (or their content) that are not owned by the publisher.

First Edition: June 2014
Originally published in 2010 as *Vidia Takes Charge*
by Random House Children's Books, a division of Random House, Inc.

Vidia Takes Charge was written by Melissa Lagonegro and illustrated by the Disney Storybook Art Team.

Library of Congress Control Number: 2013050906

ISBN 978-0-316-28337-3

10 9 8 7 6 5 4 3 2 1

CW

Printed in the United States of America

Passport to Reading titles are leveled by independent reviewers applying the standards developed by Irene Fountas and Gay Su Pinnell in *Matching Books to Readers: Using Leveled Books in Guided Reading*, Heinemann, 1999.

Meet Vidia

Adapted by Celeste Sisler

LITTLE, BROWN AND COMPANY
New York • Boston

Attention, Disney Fairies fans!
Look for these words when you read
this book. Can you spot them all?

butterfly

crickets

cage

cat

Tinker Bell and the fairies
fly to the Mainland
to get ready for summer.

One fairy paints lines and dots
on a butterfly.
Other fairies teach crickets
how to sing!

Tink and Vidia fly high
above a tree.
They see a car drive by and
follow it.

Two humans get out of the car.

Tink gets close to hear them.

"I wish it were summer all year long,"
says the girl.

"Yes, Lizzy," says her father.

They go inside the house.

Tink and Vidia fly around
to the backyard.
They see a fairy house.
Lizzy must have made it.
"Wow," says Tink.

Tinker Bell goes inside.

"This could be a trap!"

Vidia shouts.

"It is safe," says Tink.

Vidia slams the door
as a joke.

It sticks shut!

Tink is trapped inside!

Lizzy goes outside and finds

Tink in the fairy house.

She brings her inside.

Vidia flies to a window.

She sees Tink in a cage.

She also sees a mean cat!

Vidia races back to the fairies.

She says Tinker Bell

needs their help.

Clank and Bobble

will make a boat.

Vidia leads the way,

and the fairies set sail.

They come to a waterfall.

The boat goes down!

They work together and

make it to the shore safely.

Vidia finds a road.

She takes a step and

gets stuck in the mud!

The fairies help pull her out.

Vidia is sad.

She feels bad for Tink.

"This is not your fault," says Rosetta.

They will save Tink together!

"Faith, trust, and pixie dust!"

they shout.

The fairies sneak into
Lizzy's house.
The cat jumps out!
The fairies run fast
and get away.

Vidia finds Tink in Lizzy's room.

She learns that Tink and Lizzy

are now friends!

Lizzy frees Tink.

The new friends
have a picnic.
Vidia is happy that
Tink is safe.
The fairies go home.